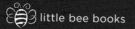 little bee books

251 Park Avenue South, New York, NY 10010
Copyright © 2018 by Little Bee Books
All rights reserved, including the right of reproduction in whole or in part in any form.
Library of Congress Cataloging-in-Publication Data
is available upon request.
Printed in China TPL 0120
ISBN 978-1-4998-0723-3 (hardcover)
First Edition 10 9 8 7 6 5 4 3 2 1
ISBN 978-1-4998-0722-6 (paperback)
First Edition 10 9 8 7 6 5 4 3 2
ISBN 978-1-4998-0724-0 (ebook)

littlebeebooks.com

For more information about special discounts on bulk purchases, please contact Little Bee Books at sales@littlebeebooks.com.

THE ALIEN NEXT DOOR

BASEBALL BLUES

by A. I. Newton
illustrated by Anjan Sarkar

little bee books

TABLE OF CONTENTS

1 THE FIRST CATCH

HARRIS WALKER AND HIS BEST FRIEND Roxy Martinez burst out the front door of Harris's house. They clutched baseball gloves, a bat, and a ball in their hands.

The sun shone brightly. The last bits of snow had melted. The first flowers had started to sprout, and a warm breeze mixed with the last of the chilly air.

"It's finally nice enough outside for the First Catch of the Year!" Harris said as he and Roxy ran to opposite sides of his front lawn.

The First Catch of the Year had been a tradition for Harris and Roxy since they were both old enough to throw a baseball.

Roxy took a few practice swings with her bat.

"I got this new bat for Christmas," she said. "I can't wait to use it!"

"And I got this new catcher's mitt," Harris said, pounding his fist into the soft leather. "Time to break it in!"

Roxy put down her bat and slipped on her glove. She picked up the baseball and threw it right into Harris's mitt. It landed with a crisp, cracking sound.

"I can't wait for tryouts!" Harris cried. "I hope I get to play catcher this year."

Harris skipped a ground ball across the lawn. Roxy took two steps to her right, then reached over to field the ball backhanded.

"And I hope I get to play shortstop," Roxy said.

"Keep making plays like that and you'll be on the team for sure!" Harris said.

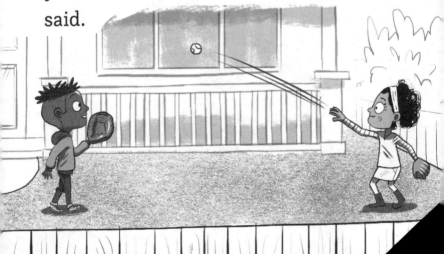

Harris and Roxy planned to try out for the Chargers, the local youth baseball team. The Chargers played against other teams from nearby towns.

Roxy tossed the ball high into the air. "Pop-up!" she yelled.

Harris looked up, raising his glove to shield his eyes from the sun. The ball started to come down.

"Hey, what are you guys doing?" asked a voice from near him.

It was Zeke, Harris's new friend and next-door neighbor, who just happened to be an alien from the planet Tragas. Harris knew his secret. Roxy did not.

"Practicing baseball," Harris replied without taking his eyes off the ball. The pop-up landed in his glove with a soft thud.

"Base . . . ball?" Zeke asked.

"You don't have baseball in Tragas?!" Roxy asked.

Harris and Roxy gave Zeke a quick explanation of the sport. They talked about pitching, fielding, hitting, and running the bases.

Zeke smiled. "This sounds a lot like a game I used to play," he said. "It's called Bonkas. Only in Bonkas, the bats are thinner and ten balls are put into play at the same time!"

"Ten balls!" Roxy exclaimed. "Boy, I have got visit Tragas some time."

"Well, it is pretty far away," Zeke said, glancing slyly at Harris.

"Hey, do you want to play catch, too?" Harris asked Zeke.

"I do," he said. "But I don't have a glove."

"No problem," said Harris. He ran into the house and brought out one of his old gloves. "You can use this."

"Play ball!" shouted Harris.

2 ZEKE AT THE BAT

"IT'S PRETTY SIMPLE, ZEKE," Harris said. "I'll hold up my glove. You try to throw the ball into it."

Zeke stood across the yard from Harris. He threw the ball. It sailed over Harris's head and landed in a neighbor's yard.

"Good try!" Roxy said, trotting over to the ball. "Now try catching."

She tossed the ball softly over to Zeke. He stuck his glove out too late and the ball bounced past him. He ran after it and picked it up.

"Now throw it to me," said Roxy holding up her glove.

Zeke unleashed another throw. This one landed across the street. "I don't know if I can do this," he said sadly.

"All it takes is practice," Harris said. "Let's keep trying."

Zeke's next few throws went onto the roof of a house, bounced off a tree, and splashed into a neighbor's swimming pool.

"Practice, huh?" Zeke said, fishing the wet ball out of the pool.

"Practice," Harris replied, smiling.

They walked back over to the yard. Zeke took a deep breath, reared back, and fired the ball right into Harris's mitt.

"That's it!" Roxy cried. "Now you're getting it!"

Zeke's next throw flew perfectly into Roxy's glove.

"You see?" she said. "You're picking this up really fast!"

But Harris wasn't so sure. Zeke may be an alien, but no one could improve that fast. *Zeke might be using his powers to control the movement of the ball,* he thought. *In a game, something like that would be cheating.*

"Let's try batting next," Harris said, hoping he was wrong about Zeke using his powers. He crouched down into a catcher's position.

Zeke picked up Roxy's new bat and took a couple of practice swings. Then Roxy threw a pitch. Zeke swung early and didn't come close to hitting the ball. It landed in Harris's mitt.

"Follow the ball in, Zeke," Roxy said. "Then time your swing."

Roxy threw another pitch. This time Zeke swung too late.

Harris could see the frustration on Zeke's face.

Zeke swung at Roxy's next pitch and smacked it high into the air. It flew over the roof and into the next yard.

"Wow!" Roxy cried. "Nice one. I want to see where that landed!" She ran off in search of the ball.

"Hey, I know what you're doing, Zeke," Harris said when the two boys were alone. "You're using your powers, aren't you?"

"What's wrong with that?" Zeke asked.

"It's a shortcut and it's cheating," Harris said. "It's not fair to the other players. You need to improve your skills through practice."

"I don't understand," Zeke said. "But I'll try."

Roxy returned with the ball. "You must have hit that 200 feet!" she said.

"Let's keep practicing," said Harris, glancing over at Zeke.

"Yes, practice," said Zeke.

3 TRYOUTS

ON THE DAY OF THE TRYOUTS, Harris, Roxy, and Zeke arrived at the field, gloves in hand.

"Harris wants to play catcher and I want to play shortstop," Roxy said. "Have you decided on a position, Zeke?"

"Since we first played, I've been watching a lot of baseball on TV," Zeke said. "I would like to be a pitcher."

"Great!" said Harris. "I hope we all make the team."

Roxy trotted out to short. Zeke stood out on the pitcher's mound. And Harris crouched behind home plate, ready to catch Zeke's pitches.

The first batter stepped into the batter's box. She raised the bat above her shoulders and stared out at Zeke. Behind the plate, Harris held up his glove.

Zeke threw his first pitch. It sailed over the batter's head and crashed into the wooden backstop.

"Just focus on my glove, Zeke," Harris shouted.

Zeke's next pitch bounced in the dirt in front of home plate. Harris slid to his right and made a great play to grab the ball before it went past him.

Harris looked out and saw the frustration on Zeke's face. "It's okay, you'll get the next one over, Zeke," he shouted, pounding his mitt a few times with his fist.

Zeke stared at Harris, then threw his next pitch—a big curveball that started way outside, then swept in a huge arc back over the plate. Everyone gasped. It was a perfect pitch!

Zeke's pitch after that did the same thing, but curved in the opposite direction this time. Then he threw a speeding bullet of a fastball that was also a perfect strike.

Harris sighed beneath his catcher's mask. *He's using his powers again*, he thought. *He has to be.*

The next batter hit a ground ball to shortstop. Roxy scooped up the ball and made a perfect throw to first base to get the runner out.

Now at bat, Harris smacked a solid hit to left field. Roxy hit a screamer to right field.

Then Zeke's turn at bat came. He stepped in to bat left-handed. Zeke swung wildly and missed the first two pitches. "Isn't he a righty?" a kid asked. *That's strange*, Harris thought. The pitcher laughed, and Zeke looked embarrassed.

"Remember, Zeke, keep your eye on the ball all the way in!" Harris shouted.

Zeke stared out at the pitcher and gripped the bat tightly. On the next pitch, he used his powers to bring the ball right to the bat.

CRACK!

Zeke's swing sent the ball flying high and deep. It sailed over the outfield fence for the only home run of the day.

"Wow! Way to hit, Zeke!" Roxy shouted.

Everyone on the field cheered as Zeke rounded the bases and crossed home plate.

Everyone except Harris.

The tryout ended and the coach read out the names of the players who had made the team. Harris, Roxy, and Zeke all made it.

"All right! We're going to be on the team together!" Roxy shouted, patting Harris and Zeke on the back.

As the three walked off the field, Harris whispered to Zeke, "We have to talk!"

4 CHEATER?

"I KNOW WHAT YOU DID BACK THERE," Harris said softly when he and Zeke were away from Roxy and the other players.

"It's not a big deal, Harris," Zeke replied. "I'm just using my natural abilities like everyone else."

"But you're *not* like everyone else," Harris said. "That's the point. Using your powers means that you're not learning how to play the game correctly or improve your skills like everyone else."

Zeke looked away.

Harris continued. "Besides, don't you think that using your powers in front of so many people is risky? Aren't you worried that someone might discover your secret? And you took a spot away from someone who deserved it. Promise me you won't use them anymore for baseball."

Harris could tell from the expression on Zeke's face that he hadn't really considered this. "Okay, I promise," Zeke said quietly and walked away.

Over the next few days, Zeke hardly said a word to Harris. For the first time since they became friends, Harris felt a strain in their friendship.

One afternoon after school, Harris decided to talk to Roxy.

"I'm worried about Zeke," he said as they tossed ground balls to each other.

"What do you mean?" she asked, snagging the ball with her glove. "He's been playing well at practice, and everyone on the team seems to really like him."

"I think he may be cheating," Harris said, realizing that he was walking a fine line between helping his friend and guarding Zeke's secret.

"Cheating?!" Roxy said, throwing the ball back to Harris. "Why do you think he's cheating?"

"Um, I'm not sure," Harris said. "But how can someone who never played baseball before suddenly be so good?"

Roxy shook her head. "That doesn't mean he's cheating, Harris. He did say he played a similar game in Tragas, Bonkers or something, so it's probably just that. I think you're a little jealous," she said. "But, now that you mention it, it's pretty amazing that Zeke seems to only throw strikes when he's pitching and hit the ball farther than everyone else—batting both left- and right-handed!"

"That's what I mean," Harris said, tossing the ball high into the air.

"Yeah, it is kind of hard to explain," Roxy said catching the pop-up.

It sure is! Harris thought. *That is, without telling you that Zeke is an alien!*

5

PLAY BALL!

THE DAY OF THE FIRST GAME for the Chargers arrived. Harris, Roxy, and Zeke took the field with their teammates.

The Chargers were playing the Scrappers. Their first batter stepped up to the plate.

"All right, Zeke, here we go!" Harris shouted.

Zeke threw his first pitch. It was way outside. Harris reached out and made a nice catch. The next three pitches also missed by a lot. The batter trotted down to first base with a walk.

"Remember, just focus on my glove!" Harris yelled out to Zeke. "That's your target. Let's go!"

But Zeke had no better luck with the next two batters. He walked each of them on four pitches. The bases were now loaded with nobody out.

Harris called time-out and ran over to Zeke.

"I'm doing what you asked," Zeke said. "I'm playing without using my powers, and look what's happening."

"You're getting a lot better with every pitch, so just try to relax," said Harris. "You'll get the next batter!"

Zeke's next pitch almost flew over Harris's head. He had to stand up and jump to catch it.

Zeke turned his back to the plate. When he turned back around, Harris saw a serious, determined look on his face.

Harris put down one finger, the signal for Zeke to throw a fastball. Zeke nodded, then fired a blazing pitch right over the plate. The batter swung late and missed. The ball slammed into Harris's glove with a thunderous crack for everyone to hear.

"Strike one!" the umpire cried.

The home crowd cheered.

"Come on, Zeke!" shouted Harris's dad from the bleachers.

But Harris was suspicious. *How could Zeke find his control so quickly?* he wondered. *And how did he throw it so fast?*

Harris signaled for the same pitch to see if Zeke could do it twice in a row. He did. Right in the same spot.

"Strike two!" the umpire yelled.

Harris was pretty sure that Zeke was using his powers again. He put down two fingers, signaling for a curveball. *Zeke hasn't been able to throw a curveball yet without cheating. Let's see what he does here*, Harris thought.

Zeke threw a perfect curveball. It looked like it was going to hit the batter—she leaned away from the pitch—but then the ball curved back over the plate.

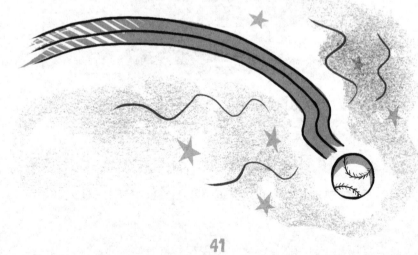

"Strike three. Yer out!" called the umpire.

Harris was now certain that Zeke using his powers.

"Way to go, Zeke!" Roxy shouted from shortstop.

Mixing fastballs in with curveballs, Zeke easily struck out the next two batters and didn't allow a run to score. As the Chargers headed for the dugout, he headed for the bench with a smile on his face.

Once Zeke sat down and took off his glove, Harris pulled him aside. "You promised," he whispered.

"I'm playing to the best of my ability," Zeke said, looking away. "That's what I'm doing. Nobody else seems to mind."

Roxy walked past Zeke. "Nice job pitching!" she said. "You're up to bat now. Get a hit!"

"See?" Zeke said to Harris, standing up and grabbing a bat.

"Could you please try to hit without using your powers?" Harris asked. "Just try."

Zeke said nothing and strode quietly to the plate.

6

SUPERSTAR!

ZEKE STEPPED INTO THE BATTER'S BOX.
He glanced over at Harris and nodded,
tight-lipped. He turned and stared at
the pitcher.

Harris took this as a sign that Zeke
had decided not to use his powers.
He watched anxiously as the pitcher
threw her first pitch.

Zeke swung wildly. He didn't even coming close to hitting the ball. The same thing happened on the next pitch, and the one afterward. Three swings, three strikes. Zeke was out.

Harris was up next. As he walked to the plate, he passed Zeke heading back to the bench with his head down.

"Good try, Zeke," Harris said. "Don't worry, you'll get a hit next time."

Zeke said nothing and sat down.

Harris lined the first pitch he saw into left field. After him, the Chargers got a bunch of hits. By the time the inning ended, they had scored three runs.

Back out on the mound, Zeke continued to play without using his powers. His pitching was slowly getting better, but the Scrappers still managed to score three runs to tie up the game.

"You're doing good out there, Zeke," Harris said as the two friends sat on the bench.

"But they tied the game," Zeke pointed out.

"It doesn't matter," said Harris. "Your pitching is getting better each inning." And then, lowering his voice, he added: "without any 'extra help.'"

It was Zeke's turn at bat again. And again he swung and missed at three pitches in a row.

Zeke headed back out to the mound. Harris could see the frustration mounting on his face.

"Forget about striking out, Zeke," Harris shouted as he took his position behind the plate. "Let's just get these next three guys out."

Zeke pitched well, but the Scrappers scored a run to take a 4–3 lead heading into the bottom of the final inning.

The first two batters for the Chargers made two quick outs. With nobody on base, Roxy came up to bat.

"C'mon now! Keep it alive, Roxy!" Harris shouted.

Roxy hit the first pitch to right field for a single.

"Yeah!" cried Harris.

Zeke was up next. The game was on the line.

"Just focus, Zeke," Harris said. "You can do it!" Harris was worried that Zeke might use his powers again.

Zeke stepped into the batter's box.

"Do your best, Zeke!" Roxy shouted as she took her lead off first base.

My best, Zeke thought. *Yes, I will do my best.*

The pitcher threw a pitch. Using his powers, Zeke directed the ball right toward his bat. He swung and smacked the ball deep to left field. The ball sailed over the fence for a two-run home run. Zeke had won the game for his team!

All the Chargers rushed onto the
field. They waited as Zeke rounded the
bases. Then the whole team jumped
up and down in a big pile at home
plate with Zeke in the middle.

Everyone except Harris.

"I knew you could do it, Zeke!" Roxy shouted. "You're a superstar!"

I can't join the celebration, Harris thought, *not when Zeke's a cheater!*

7
TIME TO TALK

THE CROWD OF HAPPY PLAYERS
headed off the field. That's when Roxy
noticed that Harris wasn't celebrating
with the rest of the team.

"Are you really so jealous of Zeke
that you can't even be happy for him?"
she asked, walking over to Harris. "I'm
surprised at you, Harris. I really am."

Harris looked away. He didn't know what to say.

I obviously can't tell Roxy the truth, he thought. *I promised to keep Zeke's secret, even if it costs me his friendship. And I can't celebrate Zeke's cheating and make it seem like I think it's okay for him to use his powers.*

He remained silent.

Roxy rolled her eyes, and stormed off with saying anything else.

Harris met up with his parents in the bleachers.

"What a great win for the Chargers!" his mom said excitedly. "You played so well! And we're so happy for Zeke. He's fitting in and everyone on the team seems to really like him."

"He did good, yeah," Harris said, as they all walked to his parents' car.

"You don't seem all that happy about the game," his dad said.

"No, I'm happy," Harris said. "I'm glad our team won the game and I'm glad Zeke did okay."

"Honey, are you sure you're okay?" his mom asked.

"I'm fine, Mom," Harris said.

I can't talk to anyone about what's really bothering me, he thought. *Anyone, that is, except Zeke!*

After dinner that evening, Harris decided to try to talk to Zeke. He went next door to his house.

"Hello, Harris," said Zeke's father, Xad, answering the door.

"It is nice to see you," said Zeke's mother, Quar. "We are very glad that you have taught Zeke all about bases and balls."

"Yes, he likes this game very much," added Xad.

Harris smiled and nodded, then walked over to his friend. He found Zeke, fingertips on the sides of his head, mind-projecting his homework onto a big screen that hovered above a desk.

"Are you here to tell me to stop using my powers again?" Zeke asked, turning away from the screen.

"I'm here because you're my friend," Harris replied. "And I still think you're not playing fair."

"I'm confused," Zeke said. "My understanding of cheating, as people on Earth use the term, is breaking the rules. I didn't break any rules."

"Well, you're not actually breaking a rule, because there is no rule about aliens using their powers. How could there be?" Harris asked.

"You have never had a problem with me using my powers before when I was careful—like when I saved the camper who fell out of a tree at Beaver Scouts camp. Or when I used my powers to avoid getting hit by a sack of flour at the costume contest. Why is this any different?" Zeke asked.

"I'm not sure," Harris said. "I just know that it is."

"I'll be very careful, Harris. No one will find out," Zeke said.

Harris headed home, frustrated and worried more about his friendship with Zeke than about Zeke using his powers.

Over the next few games, Zeke continued to use his powers. He pitched great and got hit after hit. The Chargers kept winning. He quickly became the most popular player on the team. He teammates even nicknamed him "Superstar."

Everyone was thrilled. Everyone except Harris.

I've never been so miserable about my team winning games, Harris thought. *And I don't know what to do about it!*

8
TAKE ME OUT . . .

HARRIS CONTINUED TO WORRY about the future of their friendship.

One afternoon, on the ride home following another Chargers victory, Harris's parents surprised him.

"How would you like to go to see the Newtown Knights?" his mom said, holding up a handful of tickets.

Harris's mood sank again. He felt nervous. He really hadn't spent much time with Zeke lately, apart from on the field.

"Great," he said half-heartedly.

About a week later, Harris, Roxy, and Zeke piled into the backseat of Harris's parents' car. His mom and dad rode up front.

"I can't wait to see Dylan Williams," Roxy said. "He's my favorite player."

"Why do you like Dylan Williams so much?" Zeke asked.

Even Zeke, seeing a professional baseball stadium for the first time, was moved by the sight—the lights shining brightly on the field, the buzz of the crowd, and the smells of hot dogs, pretzels, and peanuts.

"Snack time!" said Harris.

"Price's Pretzels!" Roxy shouted.

"Price's Pretzels?" asked Zeke.

"It's a ballpark tradition," explained Roxy. "Come on. We'll show you."

The three friends hurried to the concession stand. They each bought a huge pretzel.

"I have never had a pretzel before," said Zeke.

Harris covered his pretzel with mustard. Roxy smothered hers with cheese instead.

"It's best with mustard," said Harris.

"No way!" said Roxy. "It's *much* better with cheese!"

Zeke stared at his pretzel, then he looked at the container of mustard and the tub of cheese. He squeezed mustard all over his pretzel, then dumped half the tub of cheese on top of that and took a bite.

"Mmm, I like pretzels," he said with his mouth full.

Roxy and Harris laughed and they all headed to their seats.

The Knights took the field. Roxy jumped to her feet and cheered as Dylan Williams trotted out to his position.

"PLAY BALL!" shouted Harris's dad.

"We've loved taking you to see the Knights ever since you were little," his mom said.

"That's where I learned to love baseball!" Harris replied, feeling his mood lifting for the first time in a while.

"And we got enough tickets for Roxy and Zeke to come, too!" his dad added.

The Newtown Knights were the local professional minor-league team. Many players from the Knights went on to play in the major leagues. Their stadium was just a few miles from where Harris lived.

"Wow!" Harris said, smiling for the first time in days. "That's so cool!"

9
DYLAN IN ACTION

THE FIRST BATTER HIT A BALL sharply on the ground toward shortstop. Dylan Williams dashed to his left, dove toward second base, and stuck out his glove. He snagged the ball, then popped back up to his feet. He turned and fired the ball to first base in time for the out.

"Yeah, Dylan!" shouted Roxy. "You're the best!"

In the bottom of the inning, Dylan
lined a ball that dropped in for a hit.

"Watch him now," Roxy said to Zeke.
"He's going to try to steal second."

The next batter stepped up to the
plate. Dylan took a few steps off of
first. The moment the pitcher started
to throw the pitch, Dylan took off for
second base.

"There he goes!" Harris shouted.

The catcher threw the ball to the second baseman. Dylan slid into the base.

"Safe!" the umpire shouted.

The crowd roared.

"He did it!" Roxy cried. "He really is the best!"

"I read that Dylan practices stealing more than a hundred times a day, every day," Harris's dad said.

"I'm sorry," Zeke said. "I've been thinking about what Dylan said. I realize that even though using my powers is natural to me, it does give me an unfair advantage. I can see why it was cheating. And you're right, I need to be more careful with using my powers."

"You're going to be a good ballplayer . . . just by working hard," Harris said.

"I will work on my skills," Zeke said. "But I'm nervous about our big game."

"Only one thing to do," Harris said. "Let's go practice!"

10 ZEKE, A WINNER

FOR EACH OF THE NEXT FEW DAYS,
Harris and Zeke practiced for hours.
Zeke was now throwing more strikes.
And when hitting, Zeke learned to be
patient and time his swings.

They arrived at the team office where Dylan Williams was waiting. He was still wearing his dirty uniform.

"Nice to meet you kids," Dylan said, shaking each of their hands.

"We all play together on our local youth league team, the Chargers," Harris said.

"That's great, what positions do you play?" Dylan asked.

"I'm a catcher," Harris said. "Zeke is our pitcher."

"And I'm the shortstop, like you!" Roxy said nervously.

Dylan gave a friendly laugh. "You certainly carry yourself like a shortstop!"

Roxy smiled and blushed.

"So, how's your team doing?" Dylan asked.

"Really?!" Roxy asked excitedly.

"Really," said Harris's dad. "One of my business associates is friendly with the owner of the Knights. He set it up so we can meet Dylan. Come on!"

"I can't believe I'm going to meet Dylan Williams!" Roxy said as the group made their way down to the team office.

"Not bad for your first game, huh, Zeke?" Harris said.

Zeke smiled and nodded.

The next player singled and Dylan scored from second base.

Zeke smiled and looked around at the cheering crowd. "This is really fun," he said.

The Knights won the game and Dylan had an all-around great day: hitting, fielding, and stealing bases.

"I have a surprise for you guys," Harris's dad said. "How would you kids like to meet Dylan Williams?"

Harris and Zeke looked at each other in surprise.

"Thanks so much, Dylan," said Roxy, beaming.

Dylan held up his hand and gave each of them a high five and an autographed baseball.

On the way to the car, Zeke pulled Harris aside.

"We're having a pretty good season," Harris said. "We have a big game coming up against our rivals, the Ramblers, next week."

"Do you have any advice for young players?" Roxy asked. Harris expected Dylan to give her a few fielding or hitting or maybe baserunning tips.

"The best advice I can give you is to stay true to the sport. Never take shortcuts to win. Practice your skills and do the best you can and you'll be a winner no matter what the score is."

Harris threw a pitch, and Zeke swung and missed. On the very next pitch however, he hit the ball hard. It flew over Harris's head.

"You're getting better!" Harris said.

"Practice, practice, practice!" Zeke said, smiling.

The day of the big game against the Ramblers finally came. Zeke pitched well. But without using his powers, he gave up three runs. At the plate, he struck out his first time up, but he did manage to hit a few hard foul balls that just missed landing in the field.

In the bottom of the final inning, the Chargers started to rally back. With two outs and a runner on second, Roxy came to bat. She smacked the ball to right field, which scored the Chargers' first run.

"Nice hit, Roxy!" Zeke shouted from the bench.

Harris came up next. He also put the ball in play, scoring Roxy. The Chargers were now trailing 3–2. With Harris on second, they were just one hit away from tying the game.

Zeke came up to bat.

"Come on, Zeke! You got this!" Roxy shouted from the bench.

"Remember what we practiced!" Harris yelled from second base.

Zeke nodded, then stepped in to face the pitcher.

Zeke swung and missed at the first pitch. When the next one came, he drew back the bat, but swung and missed again.

The Chargers were now one strike away from losing.

Zeke looked out at Harris, who gave him a thumbs-up sign. Then he turned to face the pitcher.

Zeke swung at the next pitch.

BOOM!

He hit the ball hard and Harris started running as fast as he could. But the centerfielder tracked down the ball and caught it, so Zeke was out. The ball game was over and the Chargers had lost.

Everyone on the team was disappointed—everyone except Zeke, who trotted back to the bench with a huge smile on his face.

"What are *you* so happy about?" asked one dejected teammate.

"I hit the ball in play!" Zeke said. "And I did it all on my own!"

The teammate looked at him strangely, then walked away.

Harris patted Zeke on the back. He was happy, too.

"Good job," said the coach. "Now, who's ready for a pizza party!"

"When can we practice next?" Zeke asked Harris, who was thrilled that Zeke wanted to keep improving his baseball skills and that they were good friends again.

Harris laughed. "Right after we get some pizza!"

When Zeke entered the building this February morning, he was shocked by what he saw. The walls were covered with bright red and shiny paper hearts. Curly pink ribbons dangled from the ceiling.

Zeke saw pictures of babies with wings soaring through the sky shooting arrows.

I haven't met any human babies yet, Zeke thought. *Do they really have wings?*

Signs hung everywhere saying: "Be My Valentine!", "I ♥ you!", "It's *heart* not to love you!", "Be my pal-intine!"

Zeke was confused. Normally, the school hallways were filled

RED HEARTS, PINK STREAMERS

ZEKE WALKED INTO JEFFERSON Elementary School. Since his arrival on Earth from the planet Tragas a few months ago, he had started to feel more and more comfortable with Earth customs with each new day. At first, everything on this new planet seemed strange to him. Now, even something that was scary at first, like walking into school, was no big deal.

Except for today.

with posters and signs about school plays, sports competitions against other schools, or class projects. But this? This seemed unusual, even for humans.

Zeke stopped a boy who was hurrying to his first class.

"Um, excuse me, but why is all this stuff up on the walls?" he asked.

The boy shook his head, rolled his eyes, and kept walking. Looking back over his shoulder he said, "What planet are you from, man?"

"Trag—" Zeke started to answer automatically, but caught himself in time. No one but his best friend Harris Walker knew that Zeke was really an alien.

Then the boy stopped and added, "Valentine's Day is next week. What else would it be?"

"I . . . don't . . . know?" Zeke replied as the boy disappeared down the hall. "And what's Valentine's Day?"

At lunchtime, Zeke sat with Harris as he usually did. He was eager to figure out what all these strange decorations were about.

"I have a question," Zeke said. "What is Valentine's Day?"

"Ah, I guess you don't have this holiday on Tragas," Harris said, being sure to keep his voice low to protect his friend's secret.

"No, we don't," Zeke admitted.

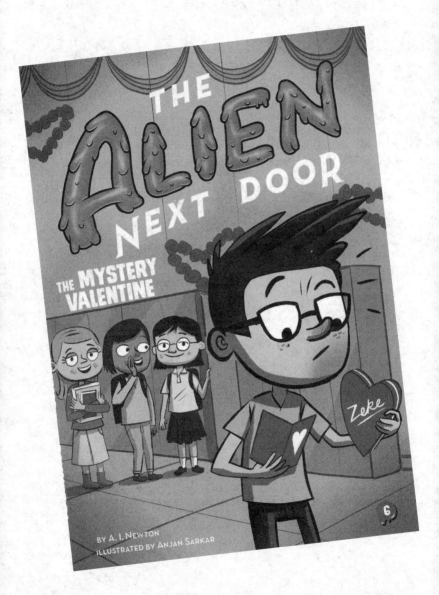

THE ALIEN NEXT DOOR

THE MYSTERY VALENTINE

Zeke

BY A. I. NEWTON
ILLUSTRATED BY ANJAN SARKAR

Read on for a sneak peek at the sixth book in the Alien Next Door series!

"Valentine's Day is a holiday when you let the people that you like know that you care about them," Harris explained. "You can give them a card, or candy, a gift, or something shaped like a heart."

"Now I'm even more confused," said Zeke. "What does the organ that pumps blood through the body have to do with liking someone?"

Harris smiled. "It's just a symbol. On Earth, the heart is the place where you feel an emotion, like love. Don't you have any similar holiday like that on Tragas?"

"Well, we have Hole-tania Day," said Zeke. "That's when each being on Tragas digs a hole and fills it with pieces of furniture they no longer want. Then they invite everyone they love over to see it."

"Um . . . okay," said Harris, a little confused now himself. "Don't worry, Zeke. It's one of those things that might be easier to just experience than to explain. You'll get the hang of Valentine's Day!"

Journey to some magical places, rock out, and find your inner superhero with these other chapter book series from **Little Bee Books**!

A. I. NEWTON always wanted to travel into space, visit another planet, and meet an alien. When that didn't work out, he decided to do the next best thing—write stories about aliens! The Alien Next Door series gives him a chance to imagine what it's like to hang out with an alien. And you can do the same—unless you're lucky enough to live next door to a real-life alien!

ANJAN SARKAR graduated from Manchester Metropolitan University with a degree in illustration. He worked as an illustrator and graphic designer before becoming a freelancer, where he now gets to work on all sorts of different illustration projects! He lives in Sheffield, England.

anjansarkar.co.uk

LOOK FOR MORE BOOKS IN THE *ALIEN NEXT DOOR* SERIES!